Otto and Oscar

Story by Bonnie Larkin Nims
Illustrations by Gioia Fiammenghia

SRA
Macmillan/McGraw–Hill

Product Design and Development: PAT CUSICK and ASSOCIATES
Design Director: LESIAK/CRAMPTON DESIGN INC.
Project Supervisor: DEBORAH AKERS

ISBN-002-686038-4

Otto made wishes.
  Oscar did too.
But the wishes they wished
    never came true.

3

Pop! Pop! Pop!
Up popped
  an odd little man!

bog
fog
cog
hog

"STOP!" he said.
  "I'm the Wish Doctor.
  Don't stop wishing
    until you hear my offer."

5

Said Otto,
"I wish for a DOG
    with ears that flop,
and long soft fur—
    I'd like that a lot!"

6

Said Oscar,
"A spinning TOP! . . .
    that never wobbles
and never totters
    and never stops."

Said Oscar,
"A new FISHING ROD
    and a cool, cool spot
and a box full of bait
    on a day that is hot!"

Said Otto,
"My own LUNCH BOX
filled up to the top. . .
with hot dogs
and popcorn balls
and lots of soda pop!"

9

Said Oscar,
"Lots of little FROGS
in a mossy bog.
They go hop, hop, hop
on a long wet log."

Said Otto,
"A CLOCK that tocks and ticks
and ticks and tocks
It goes fast or slow
but it never stops!"

11

Said Oscar,
"The bottom of a pond or
lots of hard rocks.
My wish is for FOSSILS
for my new Fossil Box!"

Said Otto,
"A jolly little TROLLEY
with a happy little song.
It goes 'Ding-Dong-Ding'
as it rolls along."

13

Said Oscar,
"A ROBOT that I can start and stop!
It will open my door
and mop my floor.
It will wash and dry my dirty socks!"

Then Otto and Oscar stopped!

Said the Wish Doctor,
"Ten is the number!
You need one more
or none of these wishes
will be yours!"

Poor Otto! Poor Oscar!
You heard the Wish Doctor.
Will you be their friend?
Will you wish a
    <u>short</u> <u>o</u> wish for them?